FIBBING FELICITY

by TONY GARTH

Felicity was on her way home from school. "Guess what?" she said to her friend, Stephanie, "My dad's just bought a huge speedboat and we're going for a ride later." Stephanie shook her head, Felicity was always making things up.

Felicity carried on. "If he's back, of course. He's an astronaut, and he's going to the moon today."

"I thought your dad was a vet?" said Winston.

"Yes...," said Felicity, "he's that too!" But nobody believed her.

That evening, Felicity was reading her comic.

"Have you done your homework, Felicity?" her mum asked.

"Yes, mum," she fibbed. She didn't mean to fib to her mum and she knew it was wrong. "I'll just finish my comic," she thought, "and then I'll do my homework."

But soon it was bedtime and she'd forgotten all about her homework.

The next day, Stephanie asked Felicity where her homework was. Felicity suddenly remembered that she'd forgotten to do it! "Erm..., OH!" she said.

"If you don't have a good reason, you'll get into trouble with Miss Harper," said Stephanie. Felicity had to think of something quickly.

In class, Miss Harper said, "Can I have everyone's homework, please?"

All the children did as they were told, except Felicity!

"Felicity, where's your homework?" asked Miss Harper. Everyone waited for the excuse. They knew it was going to be a huge fib!

"Well, Miss, I did finish my homework, but somebody took it," Felicity began.

"Oh?" said Miss Harper.

"Yes, Miss. These little blue aliens landed in our back garden last night and asked me what I was doing." she said. "So I told them I was finishing my homework and they took it away to study it!"
Miss Harper couldn't believe her ears!

"What were they like? asked Spike, interested. "Did they look like me?"

"Well, they had blue skin and wore silver space suits," said Felicity.

"They were very nice..., really cute and friendly. They gave me some blue, galactic chocolate!"

"Really?" asked Winston. The kids wanted to know more. Very soon, the little fib grew into a great big, HUGE one! And everyone forgot that Felicity hadn't done her homework.

The news spread and everyone heard about the space aliens. It was even on the news. Felicity loved the attention and her fib grew EVEN BIGGER...! "They're very clever," she said to the news man. "They can count to five thousand in fifty seconds and speak backwards. And, they're coming back tonight," she said. Well, everyone was thrilled to hear this!

That evening, the neighbourhood was full of people who wanted to meet the little blue spacemen. Everyone from school came, even the teachers! Felicity eagerly looked up to the sky.

"They'll be here any minute," she said into the microphone. Then suddenly, she remembered..., it was just a great big fib! "Erm..., I'm sure they'll be here soon," she said. But the kids had to go home, it was way nearly bedtime.

TV

Everyone was very disappointed. What a swizz,"
said Mr Franks.

Stella and Spike were crying. "We really wanted to
see them," they wailed.

Felicity felt awful. She had made her friends unhappy,
just because she hadn't done her homework.

"Felicity, did you make this up?" asked Sasha. Felicity felt hot and ashamed.

"No, of course not," she lied. Everyone shook their heads and left. They were upset and disappointed. At that moment Felicity decided that she would stop telling fibs. She only did it to make things more interesting, but she knew it was wrong. From now on, she would tell the truth.

The next morning, Felicity's mum was making her packed lunch. She opened up Felicity's schoolbag and, to her surprise, found her homework book, but it was empty! "Felicity," she said crossly, "you DID make up that spacemen story after all. That was a naughty thing to do!" Felicity had been caught.

"No mum, the spacemen must have come back and..., wow, look..., they kept all of my writing. It must have been soooOO GOOD!"

CALL OUR LITTLE MONSTERS INFO LINE FOR LOTS MORE: 0906 216 0066

Calls cost 25p per minute.

HOW MANY DO YOU KNOW?

BOSSY BETHANY

BOISTEROUS BILLY

CURIOUS CALVIN

CUTE CANDY

COMPUTER CHIP

CROSS CHRIS

CLUMSY CLARISSA

COMICAL COLIN

CONTRARY CONSTANCE

DANGEROUS DAVE

DIRTY DERMOT

ENERGETIC EVA

FIBBING FELICITY

FORGETFUL FIONA

FRIENDLY FRANCO

GROWN-UP GABBY

GREEDY GRAHAM

HEALTHY HEATHER

HELPFUL HENRY

IRRITATING IRVING

LAZY LARRY

KNOW-ALL NANCY

NUDE NIGEL

PICKIN' PETER

PRETEND PRISCILLA

PERFECT PRUDENCE

RUDE ROGER

REVOLTING RONNIE

SERIOUS SADIE

SECRET SAM

SMELLY SEYMOUR

SICKLY SIMON

SHY SOPHIE

SPORTY STANLEY

SPOOKY STELLA

STYLISH STEPHANIE

SULKY SUE

SILLY SYDNEY

TANTRUM TABITHA

TELL-TALE TALLULAH

TICKLISH TIMMY

TOO-LATE TOBY

TV TREVOR

WIDE-AWAKE WESLEY

WORRIED WINNIE

99p

SPLASH! Publishing Ltd
The Studio, 120 High Street, South Milford,
North Yorkshire LS25 5AQ, ENGLAND.

ISBN 1-900207-88-5